Marvellous Manners

Cowboys
Can Be
Kind

Timothy Knapman

Illustrated by **Jimothy Oliver**

NB

NEW BURLINGTON

Cowboys should be **brave** and **true**,
for that is the cowboy way.

But Cowboy Jack was **not** like that...
...until one special day.

Way out West in the playground,
Jack rode his cowboy bike.

He said, "I'll go wherever **I want**, and I'll pedal as fast as **I like!**"

He **didn't care** about honest folk,
who played like **good** girls and boys.

Without warning he'd **shoot** right past them –
and **scatter** their games and toys!

He took people's things without asking
and shouted, **"You can't catch me!"**

He **laughed** when he let go of Lily's balloon and it got stuck in a tree.

Then the day came when Jack saw a puddle next to Eve in her **brand new dress**.

And he thought, **"I'd love to splash her!"**
And then – well, can you guess?

Jack was pedalling towards **that puddle**
when, just a few metres ahead...

...a **naughty** boy went cycling by, and he splashed Jack **instead!**

Eve pointed at Jack, who was **dirty** and **wet**, and she gave him a piece of her mind.

"It **serves** you jolly well right," she said,
"for being so very **unkind!**"

"I never knew that it **felt** this **bad**," said Jack.
"I was **just** having fun!"

So he went round to everyone saying **sorry**
for all the **mean things** he'd done.

From then on Jack was **different**,
and did what a cowboy should.

He was **friendly** and joined in the games –
he was **kind** and **helpful** and **good**.

In no time at all he had plenty of **friends** - he couldn't stop **smiling** all day.

There were races to run and swings to be swung and so many **fun things** to **play!**

If you're ever way out West in the playground
and see Jack, I think that you'll find,
he's a cowboy who's **brave** and **true** -
he's a **cowboy who can be kind!**

Next steps

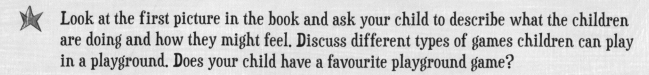

- Look at the first picture in the book and ask your child to describe what the children are doing and how they might feel. Discuss different types of games children can play in a playground. Does your child have a favourite playground game?

- Ask your child what they know about cowboys – for example, where they live, what they look like, what they wear.

- Talk about Jack's naughty behaviour and its effect on other children and on himself.

- Discuss the moment that makes Jack change the way he treats others. Why does he decide to change? Does he feel sorry for other children now that he understands how bad he made them feel?

- Ask your child to give examples of unkind behaviour and examples of friendly behaviour. What different consequences do these behaviours have? You could even use role play to show the difference between unfriendly and friendly ways of behaving.

- Explain that selfish, unkind and bad behaviour will drive away other children, which might make your child feel lonely. Talk about the fact that being kind and considerate makes it more fun to play with others and easier to make friends. Also mention that even a strong and brave child can be kind and friendly, and say sorry.

- Emphasize that the way children behave towards others can affect the way they feel. It also affects how other people treat them, and whether others like them or not.

Quarto
Knows

Quarto is the authority on a wide range of topics.
Quarto educates, entertains and enriches the lives of
our readers—enthusiasts and lovers of hands-on living.
www.quartoknows.com

A NEW BURLINGTON BOOK
First published in hardback in the UK in 2012
by QED Publishing
Part of The Quarto Group,
The Old Brewery, 6 Blundell Street
London, N7 9BH

Editor: Alexandra Koken
Designer: Andrew Crowson
Consultant: Cecilia A. Essau
Professor of Developmental Psychopathology
Director of the Centre for Applied Research and
Assessment in Child and Adolescent Wellbeing,
Roehampton University, London

A catalogue record for this book is available from the British Library.

ISBN 978 1 78171 018 0

Printed in China